This book belongs to

Gillian
Boyle

The Bureaucats

Richard Adams

Illustrated by Robin Jacques

VIKING KESTREL

VIKING KESTREL

Penguin Books Ltd, Harmondsworth, Middlesex, England
Viking Penguin Inc., 40 West 23rd Street, New York, New York 10010, U.S.A.
Penguin Books Australia Ltd, Ringwood, Victoria, Australia
Penguin Books Canada Ltd, 2801 John Street, Markham, Ontario, Canada L3R 1B4
Penguin Books (N.Z.) Ltd, 182–190 Wairau Road, Auckland 10, New Zealand

First published 1985

Printed in Great Britain by
Richard Clay (The Chaucer Press) Ltd, Bungay, Suffolk
Filmset in Monophoto Photina by
Northumberland Press Ltd, Gateshead

British Library Cataloguing in Publication Data

Adams, Richard, 1920–
The bureaucats.
I. Title   II. Jacques, Robin
823'.914[J]   PR6051.D345
ISBN 0–670–80120–8

To

Sarah Abrahams,

with love

Acknowledgement

I would like to thank my secretary,
Mrs Elizabeth Aydon,
for her patience and accuracy
in typing the manuscript.

Contents

I

The Christmas Tree

This is Richard Kitten.

This is Thomas Kitten.

This is Master.

R ichard and Thomas Kitten lived with Master and looked after the house for him.

Every day, except at week-ends, Master used to go to the Office, where he was quite grand and important. When the kittens asked him what he did there, he said, 'I work hard; I'm a Bureaucrat.'

'Well, we work hard, too, don't we,' said Thomas Kitten, 'looking after the house? So we must be Bureaucats. It sounds grand, anyway.'

One Saturday, a week or two before Christmas, it began to snow. It got quite deep. Richard and Thomas were outside, playing in the snow, when the postman came with an important-looking letter for Master. They took it indoors and gave it to him.

Master opened the letter. 'Whatever is it, Master?' asked Richard Kitten. 'It looks exciting.'

'It's an invitation to the children's ward party at the hospital,' said Master. 'They want me to be Father Christmas and give away the presents from the Christmas tree.'

'How splendid! Are we going to help?' asked Thomas Kitten. He felt most excited. 'We can dress up as very small reindeer –'

'With bells,' put in Richard.

'Plastic horns!' said Thomas, 'and harness made of –'

'No, I'm sorry,' said Master firmly. 'I'm afraid they haven't invited you.'

'Oh, Master,' cried Richard Kitten, 'that's dreadful! Can't you ask them to let us come?'

'Oh, no,' answered Master, 'I couldn't do that. You can't ask to go to a party you haven't been invited to.'

Richard and Thomas felt terribly disappointed. Several times, during the next few days, they begged Master to ask the hospital whether they couldn't go. But it was no use. Master wasn't cross or unkind: he just said No, they hadn't been invited and that was all there was to it.

The day came. Richard and Thomas helped Master to dress up as Father Christmas.

'I promise I'll bring you back something nice,' he
said, 'and that's the best I can do.'

The hospital had sent a taxi. Master got in and
drove away, with the kittens waving good-bye.

19

As soon as he had gone, Thomas Kitten turned to Richard. 'Now!' he said. 'We *are* going to the party!'

'But how?' asked Richard Kitten. 'They'll never let us in.'

'Oh, yes, they will,' said Thomas. 'I'm not a Bureaucat for nothing. I've got a secret plan! Go and get two labels and some good, thick rubber bands from Master's desk and come with me.'

It wasn't very far to the hospital. When the kittens got there they went cautiously round to the back.

Here they found a young man in a white coat who was arranging bandages and instruments on a trolley and talking to a nurse in a strong Scotch accent. Richard and Thomas, who were proud of being descended from a cat which had belonged to the Black Douglas, felt sure he would be friendly. They asked him the way to the children's ward.

They went along what seemed like miles of corridors. At last they found themselves in a sort of little hall, with two or three rooms on each side and the double doors of the children's ward at the far end. The double doors were shut, but they could hear the party going on inside. The children and the nurses were singing carols.

Suddenly the kittens heard someone coming.

'Quick!' said Thomas. 'In here!' They dashed into one of the little side-rooms.

Inside was the Christmas tree. It was huge, and all covered with coloured lights and toys – dolls and teddy-bears and engines and games and bouncing balls and boxes of bricks. It was standing on a hospital trolley, ready to be wheeled into the ward as soon as the carols were over.

'Now,' said Thomas Kitten, 'we're going to climb up it.'

'Whatever for?' asked Richard.

'I'll show you,' answered Thomas. He climbed up to the very top, fastened himself just below the big star with two of Master's rubber bands, and then tied a label round his neck. As long as he kept still he looked just like a toy animal.

Richard Kitten did the same, except that he stopped half-way up. Just then they heard footsteps outside. Both kittens kept absolutely still, with their faces fixed in what they hoped were amiable smiles.

Two nurses came in and wheeled the Christmas tree out of the door and into the children's ward. The children, who were all sitting up in their beds, clapped and cheered. Thomas Kitten, looking down from the top of the tree, felt very high up – almost as though he were on a roof.

Master, in his Father Christmas outfit, was standing in the middle of the ward with a pair of steps and some scissors. He began cutting the presents off the tree and taking them round to the children. Everyone got very excited.

Suddenly Master caught sight of Richard Kitten half-way up the tree. He stopped, and stared at him very hard. Richard Kitten kept perfectly still, smiling his amiable smile.

'How very strange!' said Master to one of the nurses. 'Do you know, that looks just like one of my own kittens at home?'

'Well,' answered the nurse, 'after all, one black kitten looks very much like another, don't you think? But I agree it's very lifelike.'

'There's no name written on the label, though,' said Master. 'I wonder who it's meant for.'

'Why not give it to little Joanna Grey, over there,' replied the nurse. 'She only came in this morning, and we always keep one or two spare presents for the newcomers.'

'Splendid!' said Master. He snipped through Richard's rubber bands and took him down off the tree. Richard Kitten held himself very stiff and went on smiling like anything. Master handed him to Joanna.

'Oh, what a lovely pussy!' cried Joanna. 'He's exactly like a real one!' And she hugged him tight.

'Y E - O W !' yelled Richard Kitten.

Everyone got the shock of their lives.

Just then there came another yowl from the top
of the Christmas tree.

'Ow! Ow! Take me down! There's a pine needle
sticking up my bottom!'

'Have we all been bewitched?' asked the head
nurse.

'Not bewitched,' said Master grimly, 'just bam-

boozled. Thomas Kitten, come down at once! I've got
something to say to you, my cat!'

'I *can't* come down, Master!' said Thomas. 'You'll
have to climb up and cut me off the tree. Oh, do hurry
up! This pine needle –'

All the children were laughing and cheering.
They thought it was a huge joke.

'What clever kittens!' said the head nurse. 'Oh, you mustn't be cross with them!'

Just then an important hospital doctor came in to see how the party was getting on. When they told him what had happened he laughed and laughed.

'Brilliant! What resourceful animals! We call that "cataplectic", you know. Of course they must stay for the party. Nurse, please give them each a saucer of milk. You're very lucky, sir, to have two such remarkable animals! Very lucky indeed!'

Joanna was given a beautiful doll instead of Richard Kitten.

The party was an enormous success. Richard and Thomas put on paper hats and sang a cat carol which everyone thought was splendid.

When the party was over, they went home with Master in the taxi. Everyone had said such nice things about them that he couldn't really be cross. The truth was that secretly he felt rather proud of them. Anyway, it was Christmas time, when no one gets scolded much.

But the kittens were both so tired that after supper they went straight off to sleep.

And that was all – until next time.

II

Operation
Rescue

'I'll be home for tea this evening,' said Master one day at breakfast, 'but after that I've got to go out again, to see the Mayor at his home in Dean Gardens. I shan't be very long, but it may make supper a bit later than usual.'

'We'll have something nice ready for you, then, Master,' said Richard Kitten. 'How about a good, big trout? You always like that. If you drop us off at the fishmonger's on your way to the office, we can walk back. It's always a good idea to be early, before the best fish has gone.'

Richard and Thomas had hardly left the fishmonger's when they caught sight of a ginger cat crouching under a wall.

'Who's that?' said Thomas. 'I've never seen him before, have you?'

'No, I haven't,' answered Richard. 'He looks awfully thin and miserable, doesn't he?'

'He looks frightened, too,' said Thomas. 'Let's ask him what's the matter.'

The strange cat certainly was frightened about something. When Richard and Thomas spoke to him he didn't answer and tried to slink away.

'You needn't be afraid of us,' said Thomas. 'Whatever's the matter?'

'I thought you might be something to do with the policemen,' answered the ginger cat. 'They're planning a big round-up to-night of all the stray cats in the town. They're going to put us in a van and – and – well – take us away somewhere.'

'How d'you know?' asked Richard.

'Blackie, the police station cat,' replied the stray; 'he heard the policemen planning it and told us. The policemen were saying there are too many stray cats in the town and they were going to get rid of them.'

'Why don't you run away, then?' asked Thomas.

'It's not that easy,' said Ginger. 'None of us has ever been out of the town in his life. We don't know the way; and anyhow, where could we go and what could we live on? This is the only place we know.'

'Yes, I see,' said Thomas. He thought for a little while. At length he said, 'I think we may be able to help. Do you know Dean Gardens, just up the road? Can you all be there by dark this evening? Only you *must* keep out of sight until I come and tell you.'

'I'm sure we'd be ready to try anything,' said Ginger.

That evening at tea, Master was very busy reading through some important papers before he went to see the Mayor. When the time came to go, Thomas Kitten was nowhere to be found. Richard saw the car out of the gate and then went in to start getting the supper ready.

Master parked the car in Dean Gardens, locked it

and walked off round the trees and bushes in the middle. Thomas Kitten, who had been hiding under a rug on the back seat, waited until he felt sure that he must have gone into the Mayor's house.

It is easy to get out of a locked car from inside. Thomas pulled up the rear door catch with his teeth.

Master had not locked the boot, but to get it open by himself was more than Thomas could manage. In the end he asked two children, who were playing in the square, to help him.

By this time it was quite dark. Thomas went off to find Ginger and his friends. They were hiding in the bushes. He had never imagined there would be so many.

He shut the lid of the boot by jumping on it. Then he got back into the car and locked himself in.

Master came back about twenty minutes later. He started the car, switched on the lights and drove away. He was in a hurry to get home for supper.

When he was about half-way home, Master saw
two policemen standing in the road, who signalled to
him to stop.

'Excuse me, sir; excuse me, sir,' said one of the policemen. 'Are you by any chance carrying any cats in this here car, sir?'

'*Cats*, officer?' replied Master in astonishment. 'Good gracious, why ever should you think I might be carrying *cats*? Please don't delay me: I want to get home. What's this all about, for goodness' sake?'

'Well, sir,' said the policeman, 'there was going to be a big round-up of stray cats to-night, only they've all mysteriously disappeared. The Super thinks someone must have warned them, and we've got orders to search all cars leaving the town.'

'But, officer,' said Master, 'it really is perfectly absurd to suppose that *I'd* be secretly carrying a lot of cats about in my car. Surely you know me, don't you?'

Now the fact was that both the policemen *did* know Master, and they knew that he was quite important and a friend of the Mayor; and privately they couldn't help thinking that it really *was* rather silly to insist on searching *his* car, even if they had to search all the others. So the first policeman said, 'Well, sorry to have bothered you, sir; only we've got our orders, you see. We'll leave it at that, though. Good-night, sir.'

'So I should think!' muttered Master to himself as he drove away. 'Stray cats, indeed! Whatever next?' He reached home and drove the car into the garage.

He had just got out when there came a frantic, muffled yowling from the boot. 'Help! Help! Let us out! We're suffocating!'

The boot was absolutely packed with stray cats. Master stared at them aghast. 'What – what's the meaning of this? What are you all doing in my car?'

Thomas Kitten appeared from behind him. 'Well, you see, Master, it was – er – it was like this . . .'

'Thomas Kitten,' said Master a minute later, 'are you aware that you've made me mislead and deceive the police, and that if this gets out I shall be in serious trouble and look a complete fool into the bargain?'

'Well – er – yes, Master, I suppose so; only, you see, I couldn't think what else to do.'

'They'll all have to stay shut up in the garage,' said Master firmly. 'Not a word of this must get out to anyone. Not a *word*; do you understand?'

Next morning Master drove to the neighbouring town, ten miles away, to buy cat food, so that no one in their own town should wonder why he could possibly want so much of it.

44

To begin with, he was absolutely furious with Richard and Thomas, but after a day or two, as nothing was discovered, he began to come round. The stray cats were terribly grateful and took the greatest care to be most quiet and polite. The garage, however, grew more and more messy and smelt terrible.

After a day or two the policemen, who had a great many other things to see to, stopped hunting for the cats. Master was able to find homes for a few among his friends, but most of them preferred to go unobtrusively back to the town and resume their old lives.

'Once a stray, always a stray, you know,' said Ginger, as he said good-bye to Richard and Thomas. 'It's a way of life, really: I can always rub along if only they'll let me alone.'

'Thank heavens for that!' said Master, when at last the garage was empty and he'd cleaned it up. 'I suppose I can't altogether blame you, Thomas. But now, you understand me clearly, my cat. Nothing like this is ever to happen again, do you see?'

'Oh, yes, Master,' said Thomas Kitten meekly. 'It won't, I promise.'

Nothing like that ever did happen again. But other things did.

III

The Great
Chocolate Adventure

'T o-morrow,' said Richard Kitten gravely, 'is the first of April.'

'It wouldn't be any use trying to make an April Fool out of Master, though,' said Thomas. 'He knows us. He'll be on the look-out and he'd see it coming a mile off.'

'He won't,' said Richard, 'because it's going to look as though we had absolutely nothing to do with it. The postman's promised to help: he thinks it's a huge joke.'

'A letter, you mean?' said Thomas. 'But neither of us can write.'

'Oh, much better than a letter,' said Richard. 'Look – I've got it hidden in this drawer.'

Under some towels and sheets was a large chocolate-box. It had a red bow and a beautiful picture of some horses on the lid. It looked quite new. Richard Kitten opened it carefully. It was empty.

'Where did you get that?' asked Thomas.

'From Mrs Aydon,' said Richard. 'She finished the chocolates a week or two ago and gave me the box.'

Mrs Aydon, who lived next door, was a lawyer's secretary. She was a great friend of the kittens, who sometimes ran errands for her and did her shopping.

Thomas Kitten sniffed at the box, which smelt of cardboard and chocolate.

'Come on,' said Richard. 'Let's go round to Mrs Aydon before Master comes home. There's important work to be done.'

Mrs Aydon thought Richard's plan was very funny. She helped the kittens to fill the box with pebbles, and then add some cotton wool to stop them rattling. They topped it off with a typed card saying 'April Fool!' Mrs Aydon suggested that to make it look more real when the parcel was undone, they might slip another card under the bow on the lid, saying 'With the Manufacturers' Compliments'.

They did it up with brown paper and Sellotape, and tied on a label addressed to Master.

'What about the stamps, though?' asked Thomas. 'I haven't any money; have you?'

'No, but used ones will do,' said Richard. 'Just stick them on with gum and leave the parcel here. The postman's promised to pick it up in the morning and bring it round with Master's letters.'

Next morning the kittens were careful to be upstairs when the postman came. After they had heard Master open the door and take in the parcel and the letters, they waited quite five minutes before coming down to breakfast. Master had already opened the parcel. However, he had left the chocolate-box on the hall table and was reading his letters in the kitchen. Neither of the kittens made any remark.

After breakfast Master put on his hat and coat, said good-bye as usual and drove away to the office, taking the chocolate-box with him. All that was left was the card saying 'With the Manufacturers' Compliments', which he had taken out from under the bow.

The kittens felt baffled and disappointed.

'Do you think he's guessed?' asked Thomas.

'I can't tell,' answered Richard. 'It's puzzling, isn't it? Like when you've lit a firework and you're not sure whether it mightn't have gone out.'

The day passed uneventfully. In the evening the kittens got tea ready and Master came home at his usual time. Wherever the chocolate-box might be, he certainly hadn't got it with him. He sat down and began pitching into his sardines on toast. At length Richard Kitten could contain himself no longer.

'Someone sent you some chocolates this morning, didn't they, Master?' he asked. 'Were they nice?'

'Oh – er – yes – the chocolates,' answered Master rather vaguely. 'I'd quite forgotten. Well, to tell you the truth, Richard, I gave them away. You see, I don't really care much for chocolates, and I had quite an important visitor to entertain for lunch to-day – the Countess Alicia van Zaal, from Luxemburg. She's a friend of the Mayor and she's staying in the town to-night. I gave the chocolates to her.'

'Wh-what happened, Master?' asked Thomas, staring.

'What d'you mean, what happened?' replied
Master. 'She thanked me and took them away with
her, of course.' And he went on reading the evening
paper.

Richard and Thomas Kitten stared at each other
in horror. After a few moments Richard slipped out of
the room. Thomas followed him.

'What on earth are we going to do?' whispered Richard. 'That foreign Countess will be absolutely furious! When the Mayor hears about it Master might even get the sack or something.'

'We'll have to go and find her,' said Thomas. 'With a bit of luck she may not have opened them yet. Come on, off we go – quick!'

'But where?' asked Richard.

'If she's a Countess she's sure to be at the grandest hotel in the town,' said Thomas. 'You know – the Cleverly Bilton, with the revolving doors and all the pot plants outside. Go and get an envelope out of Master's desk and bring it with you. Hurry!'

The kittens ran all the way into the town without stopping. When they reached the Cleverly Bilton they were quite out of breath and had to rest for a minute or two outside. Then Thomas led the way through the revolving doors and up to the reception desk. The lady behind it looked rather surprised, but smiled at them quite kindly.

'Good evening, madam,' said Thomas Kitten respectfully. 'Our master's sent us with a note for the Countess van Zaal.' (Richard held up the envelope.) 'We've been told to give it to her personally.'

'Oh, I see,' replied the lady. She consulted a large book on the desk. 'Ah, yes; she's in Room 539. The liftman will take you up to the fifth floor. You *are* house-trained, aren't you?' she added. To this the kittens disdained to reply.

Upstairs everything was very quiet, with long, empty corridors and thick carpets. Tiptoeing along, the kittens felt very nervous, but managed to find Room 539 without meeting anyone. There was a bell-button beside the door. Richard climbed on Thomas's back and rang it.

After a few moments the door was opened by a large, imposing lady wearing a grey silk dress and a pearl necklace. She also looked surprised to see the kittens. Glancing quickly past her into the room beyond, they could see the chocolate-box lying on the window-sill. Evidently it was still unopened.

'Good evening, your ladyship,' said Thomas Kitten, bowing most politely. 'We are the hotel rodent detectives. It's our job to visit all the rooms and make sure there are no rats or mice that might bother guests in the night. If it's not putting you to any inconvenience, may we make a quick search?'

'Oh, zat ees vairy nice!' replied the Countess graciously. She stroked Thomas's head: then she stroked Richard's head as well. 'Pray come to make your sairch! But nozzing ees to find, I sink.'

She sat down at the dressing-table and began doing her hair. Richard and Thomas, advancing into the room, crept round to the far side of the bed.

'Now!' whispered Thomas.

'A mouse! A mouse!' cried Richard. 'After it, quick!'

'Une souris? Ah, mon Dieu!' screamed the Countess. She climbed up on the dressing-table stool and buried her face in her hands.

Thomas dashed madly round the room, spitting and yowling at the top of his voice. Richard, leaping on the window-sill, pushed the chocolate-box out of the open window.

'Well done!' cried Thomas. 'It's all right, your ladyship; my colleague has caught the mouse.'

'I've eaten it, your ladyship,' said Richard. 'No mess, nothing left at all! Oh, but I'm so *sorry*! I'm afraid your chocolates have got knocked out of the window in the scuffle. I *do* apologize! Please forgive me!'

'Oh, zat ees not to mattair!' said the Countess. 'Bettair zan 'ave ze mouse, I sink! You are doing your vork ver' good! Fine poozies!'

And with this she opened her purse and handed Thomas a pound note.

'You can't beat a real lady, can you?' said Richard Kitten, as they made their way out through

66

the revolving doors. 'Let's call in at the fish and chip shop on the way home. All the same,' he added after a few moments, 'I don't think we'll try that April Fool business next year. Seems a bit risky, don't you think?'

IV

The
Conjurer's Rabbit

'W ell, I never!' said Richard Kitten, who was dusting the window-sill in Master's bedroom. 'Come and look!'

'What is it?' said Thomas, joining him at the window. 'D'you mean that dog in the road? I can't see –'

'No, no!' said Richard. 'In the next-door garden, look! There's a white rabbit on the lawn! Come on, let's go down.'

There was indeed a lop-eared, pink-eyed white rabbit on the lawn in the next-door garden. He was inside a small wire pen and was eating the grass with a rather abstracted air. Seeing Richard and Thomas looking through the fence, he became nervous.

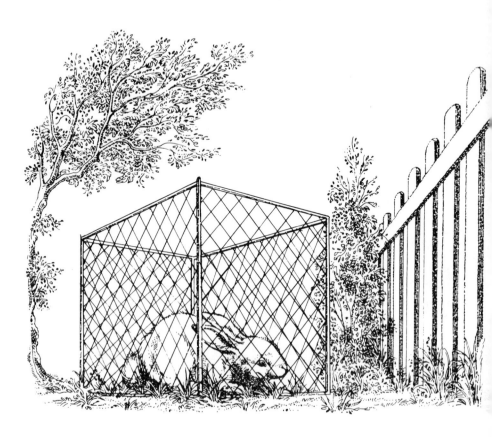

'You needn't be afraid of us,' said Thomas Kitten.
'What's your name? Have you come to live here?'

'No,' replied the rabbit. 'No such luck! My name's
Zero: I belong to the conjurer. He produces me out of
a top-hat, you know: it's part of his show.'

'Conjurer?' asked Richard.

'There's a children's party here this afternoon,'
said the rabbit. 'The conjurer's been invited to lunch,
so that he can get everything ready in time.'

'What an exciting life you must have!' said
Richard Kitten. 'Do you enjoy being produced out of
the hat?'

'No, I hate it,' replied Zero. 'Always travelling about – never any peace and quiet; and every time I have to come out of the hat I'm shut up in the dark for a long time first. It's no life for a rabbit. Besides, I don't like the conjurer,' he added. 'He's not a kind man.'

'Well, I'd absolutely love to be produced out of a hat,' said Thomas Kitten. 'Do you think I could take your place this afternoon?'

'It wouldn't be any good asking the conjurer,' answered Zero. 'He'd only say no. All the same,' he went on after a minute, 'we might be able to manage it *without* asking. He'll be awfully cross, but it'll be worth it, not to be shut up in the dark for once: that always frightens me, you see.'

'What have we got to do, then?' asked Thomas.

'Well, the conjurer has a trick table,' said Zero, 'with secret drawers and things. Before a party he always brings it into the room and gets it ready, and I have to be shut up in a hidden compartment. The top-hat has a false crown, and when he does the trick he reaches through and pulls me out.'

'But if he won't say yes?' asked Thomas.

'Well, it's a fine day,' said Zero. 'All the windows are open, look. Once everything's ready the conjurer usually goes off and has a drink in his room. You could come in through the window, let me out and get in the compartment yourself. Then I'll go off with your brother until afterwards. But you'd better go away now, before the conjurer comes back and sees us talking.'

The day stayed fine. That afternoon Richard and Thomas, hiding in the front garden, kept a careful watch on the next-door drawing-room. They could see the conjurer moving about and getting everything ready, just as Zero had said. At length he finished and went away. The kittens, running quickly across the lawn, jumped in at the open window.

The table was at the far end of the room. After several minutes' cautious fiddling, they managed to open the secret compartment. Zero was inside, looking very cramped and uncomfortable. He scrambled out and Thomas Kitten got in. Richard and Zero, having shut everything up again, slipped away through the garden.

Soon Thomas Kitten realized what Zero had meant. The compartment was pitch-dark and terribly stuffy and uncomfortable. He wished he had never had the idea.

After some time he heard the children coming in and sitting down. He could hear grown-up voices too – fathers and mothers, he supposed. Then the conjurer came up to the table and began the show. As he did his various tricks he was making jokes and the children were laughing and clapping. It seemed to go on for hours.

At last the conjurer, in a very important voice, said, 'And now I want you to watch me carefully. This, as you all can see, is a perfectly empty top-hat. I'm going to put it down here and I want you to keep your eyes on it.' But then he told another joke and did something or other (Thomas didn't know what) to distract the children's attention while he pressed the secret button to open the compartment under the hat. At the same time the crown of the hat, which was hinged, dropped down, just missing Thomas's head.

'Now,' said the conjurer, gazing all round at the
children. 'I'll bet you don't believe, do you, that there
could be a real, live rabbit inside that empty hat?'

'No!' they all answered.

'Well!' said the conjurer, pretending to do a
magic spell. 'Watch!'

Without looking down, he grabbed Thomas
Kitten with one hand, took hold of the hat with the
other (the crown was made to spring back into place)
and picked it up off the table.

'Rabbit!' he cried. 'Hey presto!' And with this he
pulled Thomas out by the scruff of his neck.

The children all roared with laughter. So did the grown-ups, too.

'Call that a rabbit?' shouted one little boy: and another one, loud enough for everyone to hear, said, 'I reckon he needs some stronger glasses, don't you?'

The conjurer was fearfully angry. Thomas Kitten was glad the children were there, because he felt sure that otherwise the conjurer would probably have hurt him. As it was, he carried him into the next room, put him into a drawer, locked it and pocketed the key. 'I shall come back and deal with you later,' he said. Then he hurried back to finish the show.

Thomas Kitten felt every bit as cross as the conjurer.

'What a beast!' he thought. 'I'm jolly well not going to give him a chance to deal with me – whatever that means. The very moment he opens the drawer I shall jump out and scratch him! Then I'll run home!'

Now while everyone was in the drawing-room watching the conjurer, a burglar, who had found out that they were having a party that day, climbed in through a back window and began going stealthily through the house, stealing anything that looked valuable. After a time he came to the library, where Thomas Kitten was shut up. He took a silver cup and a clock off the mantelpiece and then began going through the drawers.

When he found that one of the drawers was locked, the burglar naturally supposed there must be something very valuable inside: a lot of money, perhaps. He had a tool for picking locks, and after a minute or two he was able to slide the drawer open.

Thomas Kitten, who thought it was the conjurer come back, sprang out like a miniature tiger, spitting with rage and clawing at his neck and face. The burglar was taken completely by surprise. He staggered back, tripped, and fell on the floor with a crash.

The grown-ups came running in. They grabbed the burglar and telephoned for the police. The father of the children whose party it was recognized Thomas Kitten.

'You splendid cat!' he said. 'You've saved me from being robbed of all my best things! You're a hero – an absolute hero! You must have a reward: I'll give you anything you like! Come on, just ask me!'

'Please, sir,' replied Thomas Kitten, 'can I have the conjurer's rabbit?'

The conjurer tried to object, but the children's
father offered him so much money for the rabbit that
he felt he'd be silly to refuse. Thomas Kitten went
home in triumph. He and Richard spent the rest of the
afternoon cleaning out an old hutch which was up in
the garage loft. When they had finished, Zero was
installed.

When Master came home that evening, he found Zero happily nibbling one of his best lettuces, which the kittens had cut for him.

'Thomas, whatever's all this?'

'Well, you see, Master,' said Thomas, 'it was – er – well, you see, it was like this . . .'

At that moment the children's father came round himself to tell Master all about it. By the time he'd finished, Master couldn't very well say Zero couldn't stay.

'But you're *never* to do anything like that again!' he said. 'And what's more, it seems to me I'm always saying that, Thomas. Perhaps I ought to keep you both in a dungeon: then I might have a bit of peace.'

'Don't worry, Master,' said Thomas. 'That's one thing I'll *never* do again. That magic table was worse than any dungeon!'

V

The
Prize Poem

'T his will interest you both,' said Master one morning.

The kittens, who were sitting on the window-sill, watching the starlings on the lawn, turned round to see him looking at a photograph in the newspaper.

'What is it, Master?' asked Richard Kitten. 'A cat for Parliament?'

'No, no,' replied Master. 'It's a cat from Persia, come here on a visit.'

'So it is!' said Thomas, jumping up on the table to look at the photograph. 'Is that his mistress? What's it say, Master?'

'"Abu Sir,"' read Master, '"champion of Teheran, with his mistress, the Persian film actress Miss Parizade Mirza. Abu Sir and Miss Mirza are staying in London for the completion of her new film, 'The Arabian Nights'."'

'What a lot of fluffy fur he's got!' said Richard Kitten. 'Is *he* in the film, too?'

'It doesn't say,' said Master. 'But then it goes on: "To mark the occasion of Miss Mirza's visit, the *Daily Orator* is offering a prize of £1,000 for the best poem in honour of her and of Abu Sir. Entries to be submitted by the end of this week."'

'You ought to go in for it, Master,' said Richard.
'Just think –'

'Good gracious, I've got something better to do than write silly poems!' said Master. 'What's the time? Heavens, I'd no idea it was so late! Where's my hat, Richard?'

From time to time during that day the kittens talked about the beautiful actress and her Persian cat.

'D'you think she's an eastern enchantress?' said Thomas. '"The Arabian Nights" sounds awfully romantic. You could start a poem like that, couldn't you? "O fair enchantress of a thousand hearts –"'

'E'en more bewitching than thy Persian puss –' added Richard.

'– Of snowy fur, whose blue-eyed gaze imparts' (cried Thomas excitedly) 'An orient magic to thy genius!'

Thoroughly inspired, Richard Kitten climbed on the table, waving the newspaper.

'Slink through my dreams, soft-footed and sharp-clawed,
Thou and thy mistress have ensnared my heart!
She, almond-eyed, and thou, the velvet-pawed . . .'

There was a lot more of this. Finally the kittens stopped housework for the day and spent the afternoon completing and improving their poem. By tea-time it was finished, and Richard, standing on the bird-bath in the garden, recited the whole thing to Zero, who was deeply impressed.

'Come on, quick!' said Thomas. 'Let's go round and ask Mrs Aydon to type it out, before we've forgotten it all!'

'Are we going to send it in to the paper?' asked Richard.

'I don't suppose they'd accept it for the competition,' said Thomas. 'Not if they knew it was by a couple of cats. I know! Let's say it's by Master! It won't win, of course, but at least it might be one of the ones they print.'

Mrs Aydon typed the poem from Richard's dicta-
tion, and they sent it off with Master's name and
address at the foot of the page. That evening Master
took them out fishing, and they had such an exciting
time catching their supper that they forgot all about
the poem.

The week passed, and then the next week. It was beautiful weather. The kittens played in the garden, climbed trees and went for a picnic with Master on Blueberry Down.

It was nearly a fortnight later when Master, at breakfast, suddenly put down his knife and fork and stared at the newspaper.

'Good heavens!' he said. 'What's all this? "O fair enchantress of a thousand hearts, E'en more bewitching than thy Persian puss ..." '

'Oh, have they really printed our poem, Master?' cried Richard Kitten. 'How splendid! What's the winning one like?'

'That *is* the winning one!' said Master, staring at the kittens in horror. 'And they say it's by *me*! Thomas Kitten, what's the meaning of –'

'Well – er – you see, Master,' said Thomas Kitten. 'It was – er – it was like this. We – er – well, we thought, you see –'

At that moment there was a ring at the door-bell. It was a reporter from the *Daily Orator*, come to congratulate Master and write an interview for publication in the paper. Master refused to talk to him and fled to the office.

But there was no peace for him there, either. 'It's terrible!' he said to the kittens that evening. 'Everyone's saying I must be in love with Miss Parizade Mirza. They're all teasing me about it. You've made me look a complete fool!'

Next morning another reporter arrived, together with a photographer. They brought with them a pressing invitation from the editor, asking Master to go to a party in London to meet Miss Parizade Mirza and her cat. Master refused to say a word, but the photographer followed him to the office, taking pictures all the way.

'It's no good, we'll have to tell them it was us,' said Thomas Kitten to Richard. 'Poor Master! It's making him look silly at the office, where he's supposed to be grand and important.'

They went outside, caught up with the reporter just as he was getting into his car and told him all about it.

But this only seemed to make things worse. The reporter immediately wrote an article entitled 'Brilliant Kittens in Prize Poem Drama', beginning 'The amazing truth can now be revealed!' Whenever the kittens went into the garden, photographers seemed to be lying in wait. Master was ceaselessly pressed to take them to London to meet Parizade Mirza. He had to go and see the Mayor and say he was sorry, and that he hadn't known anything about the kittens' poem. The Mayor was none too pleased. He said Master ought to keep his kittens under proper control.

Next evening, just at supper time, there were no fewer than three interruptions from newspapermen at the door. After the third, Master came back into the kitchen and sat for some time in silence. At last he said, 'I'm sure I'm a patient man, but I've finally had enough! You two – you're nothing but a continual nuisance! If it's not one thing, it's another! I can't call my soul my own! I'm going to get rid of you both, and you've only got yourselves to thank for it. I shall ring up the R.S.P.C.A. Inspector, now!'

'Oh, Master!' cried Thomas Kitten.

'Be quiet!' said Master sternly. He got up and went over to the telephone.

At this moment there was yet another ring at the door-bell. Master answered it, but this time he got no chance to refuse to speak, for the visitor made his way indoors, talking as he came. He was a large person, wearing a broad-brimmed, grey hat, horn-rimmed glasses, black-and-white shoes and a very loud check suit.

'Good evening, sir; good evening! My name is Homer J. Tasker from Nebraska, sir. I am the world's greatest exhibitor of animal freaks and marvels. Cute little place you got here! Now I'm very very innerested in your poetic kittens – the only genu-ine poetic kittens in the world, or so I figure. Now I'm a plain man of business, sir, so I'll tell you straight out that I am prepared to pay fifty thousand dollars – yes, *sir* – for those two kittens in good condition. Here is my cheque, sir. Only I gotta know right away. I'm flying to Noo York to-night and I sure wanna take those kittens with me!'

A terrible silence fell. Richard Kitten noticed that Homer J. smelt of cigars and chewing-gum. He had brought a wicker basket, which he had put down on the hall floor. Thomas wondered whether to jump out of the window.

At last Master spoke. 'I'm sorry, Mr Tasker; I'm afraid my kittens are not for sale. I couldn't possibly manage without them: I need them to look after me, you see. Please accept that as quite final.'

As the front door closed behind Mr Tasker, Richard Kitten put on the kettle.

'Here are your slippers, Master,' said Thomas, 'and we've bought some nice mackerel for supper. Oh, look, there's a button missing on your cuff: I'll put on another while the kettle's boiling. I bet that Abu Sir couldn't sew on a button.'

'*Or* make up poetry,' added Richard under his breath.